Read more

MOBY SHINOBI AND TOBY TOO!

books!

Take a Hike!

Luke
Flowers

ACORN™
SCHOLASTIC INC.

To Katie Carella—thank you for being a joyful and inspiring guide on these ninjarrific adventures! I look forward to exploring a mountain of books with you, my friend. Happy trails!

Library of Congress Cataloging-in-Publication Data

Names: Flowers, Luke, author, illustrator.
Title: Take a hike! / by Luke Flowers.
Description: First edition. | New York, NY : Scholastic Inc., 2020. | Series: Moby Shinobi and Toby too ; [2] | Audience: Ages 5-7. | Audience: Grades K-1. | Summary: On a camping trip, Moby Shinobi's ninja skills keep making a mess of things but when hikers get lost he leads a team to save them.
Identifiers: LCCN 2019028597 | ISBN 9781338547542 (paperback) | ISBN 9781338547566 (library binding) | ISBN 9781338604979 (ebook)
Subjects: CYAC: Stories in rhyme. | Camping—Fiction. | Hiking—Fiction. | Ninja—Fiction. | Dogs—Fiction.
Classification: LCC PZ8.3.F672 Tak 2020 | DDC [E]—dc23 LC record available at https://lccn.loc.gov/2019028597

10 9 8 7 6 5 4 3 2 1   20 21 22 23 24

Printed in China   62
First edition, June 2020
Edited by Rachel Matson
Book design by Sarah Dvojack

Table of Contents

WELCOME TO
SHINOBI
DOJO
HIYAH-5 NINJA ARTS

Toby would like to take a hike.
The woods are something we both like!

3

Tent, compass, and a bright headlamp.
Two sleeping bags. A map of camp.

Bow and arrows, a rope to throw.
Book to read by campfire glow.

Ninjas cheer as they ride their bike.
Go Shinobi! Go take a hike!

7

Leap! Moby soars across the creek!

Shhh! Toby does a ninja-sneak!

Yes! Moose Mountain Camp, we are here!
Happy campers give a loud cheer!

Forest Friends

Our adventure has just begun.
This camp will be mountains of fun!

14

Moby thinks of a quick repair!

He has the power of a **bear.**

BEND!

POUND!

17

The smashed tents are an awful sight!
The deer agree this is **not** right!

21

27

Moby thinks of a speedy trick.

With ninja strength they will go quick!

29

31

34

You lead and I will steer our boat!

Moose power will keep us afloat!

The Shinobi team takes the lead!
They finish **first** with ninja speed!

37

Happy Trails

Time to eat at Hungry Moose Hall.
Oh no! Ranger Kate gets a call!

Hikers got lost in Lizard Park! And soon it will be getting dark!

With these tools, I know what to do!
Combine them all—make something new!

TENT

ROPE

BOW

STICKS

BELTS

44

While we took pictures of a snail, this big **tree** fell on the trail!

47

Silly bear, I am **not** afraid.
Look at all the friends I have made!

Forest friends join the wild crew!

They quickly break the tree in two.

Moby leads all the hikers back.
He lights the way to stay on track!

"You are all **safe**!" Ranger Kate cries.
She has a welcome-back surprise.

A cozy fire and yummy snacks!
There's just one thing this party lacks...

We are happy helpful ninjas
on the lookout for those in need.
HI-YAH! We always jump in
with mighty ninja speed!

About the Author

Luke Flowers lives in Colorado Springs with his wife and three children. Camping and exploring Colorado's mountains is one of their favorite activities. Once while sleeping under the stars,  Luke awoke to a nosy bear a few feet away. But the bear was just as scared as Luke was! No bear hugs were shared.

Luke has illustrated over fifty books, including *New York Times* bestseller *A Beautiful Day in the Neighborhood* by Fred Rogers. But being able to write AND illustrate the Moby Shinobi series has been the most HI-YAH-wesome highlight of his creative journey.

YOU CAN DRAW TOBY!

1 Draw a sideways heart.

2 Draw a rectangle. Add two more rectangles and a half-circle to the side of the mask. Draw the ears.

3 Add two ovals for the eyes. Fill in the pupils. Draw the nose and mouth.

4 Draw a teardrop shape to make the body. Add the tail.

5 Finish the body. Add arms and legs! Give Toby a bone!

6 Color in your drawing!

WHAT'S YOUR STORY?

Moby and Toby build a super hut.
Imagine that **you** are camping with them!
What would your hut look like?
How would you use sticks and rope?
Write and draw your story!